CLASSIC FAIRY TALES

Beauty and the BEAST

Retold by Philippa Pearce
Illustrated by James Mayhew

MACDONALD YOUNG BOOKS

This edition first published in Great Britain in 1996
by Macdonald Young Books
61 Western Road
Hove
East Sussex BN3 1JD

Designed by Shireen Nathoo Design

Typeset in 20pt Minion
Printed and bound in Belgium by Proost International Book Co.

British Library Cataloguing in Publication Data available.

ISBN: 0 7500 1996 4
ISBN: 0 7500 1997 2 (pb)

Once upon a time there was a merchant with three daughters. His two elder daughters were selfish and vain and altogether disagreeable. The youngest daughter was quite different. She was good and kind and – as you shall hear – very brave. She was so beautiful that people simply called her Beauty.

Her sisters hated her.

One day the merchant heard that a ship was expected in a far-away port with a valuable cargo for him. At once he prepared to set off on the long journey to claim his fortune. His two elder daughters made him promise to come back with expensive presents for them. Beauty, however, wanted only a rose.

The merchant rode off. But, at the end of his long journey, he was bitterly disappointed: there was no ship with valuable cargo waiting for him. That news had been false. Sadly he turned homeward again. He had no money, after all, to buy expensive presents for his elder daughters. He could not even find a rose for Beauty, for it was now too late in the season for roses.

Through wintry weather the merchant began riding home. His way took him into a great forest, and by now snow was driving down in a blizzard. Over the wind's howling the merchant heard the distant howling of wolves. He and his horse struggled on,

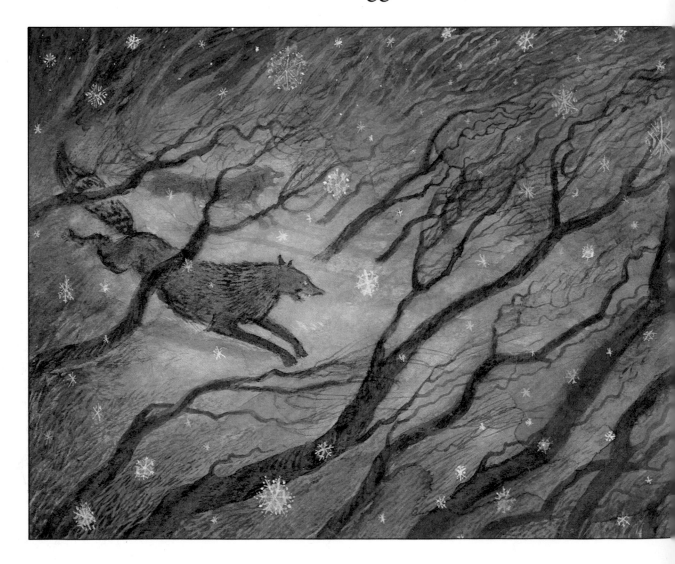

anxious, half-frozen, and – worst of all, as the merchant soon realized – lost.

At last they came to a place where the trees seemed to form an avenue, as if leading to some great house. Thankfully the merchant turned his horse this way.

As he rode down the avenue, the snow ceased to fall and the bitter wind to blow. The sun came out, birds began to sing, flowers to bloom. To his amazement, the merchant rode from winter into high summer.

At the end of the avenue, he came to a house as magnificent as a palace. He rode his horse up to steps of agate that ascended to tall doors inlaid with gold. He dismounted, went up the agate steps and knocked on the gold-inlaid doors. No one came, but the great doors swung open, as if to welcome him in. Inside he saw a huge hall, marble floored and marble walled, splendidly furnished, but empty of life.

"Is no one here?" the merchant called. Only the echo answered him: No one here ... no one here ...

"Can I come in?" he called; and again the echo answered: Come in ... come in ...

The merchant looked back at his horse: it was already moving off in the direction of the stables, to find food and water and rest. So the merchant walked boldly through the open doorway and into the great splendid empty echoing hall.

There were doors all round the hall, and
each door, as he approached it, opened before
him. Through one door he came to a room
with a supper-table laid for one. He sat down
and at once delicious food and drink
appeared before him. He reached for the
knife and fork, and at once the knife and
fork sprang into his hands.

When he had
finished his supper, the
merchant went to sleep
in the comfortable,
clean bed that was
waiting for him. In the
morning he found that
his old travel-stained
clothes had vanished;
in their place lay new
ones of the best
quality. He put them
on and found they
fitted to perfection.

Now he made his way back through the great empty echoing hall, through the tall doors inlaid with gold, and down the agate steps. There was his horse waiting for him.

The merchant was about to mount and ride off, when it occurred to him that he had not seen anything of the gardens of this enchanted palace. So he began to wander through them – along walks, across lawns, through leafy archways, until at last he came to a walk at the end of which played a fountain of high-glittering water. Beyond the fountain was a bower of roses whose scent filled the air.

The sight and smell of the roses reminded the merchant of his promise to Beauty. He reached out to pick a rose, and, as he did so, there was a shaking and a rumbling and out from the rose bushes burst a huge Beast, such as the merchant had never seen before. It had glaring eyes and snarling fangs and angry claws and bristling fur. It roared at him: "Wretched creature, who gave you leave to pick my roses?"

The merchant was dumb with terror.

The Beast said: "Last night you were my guest, and I granted your every wish. Now, this morning you steal from me the one thing I love – my roses."

The merchant managed to whisper: "Sir, I meant only to take a rose for one of my daughters."

The Beast said: "Then you have daughters – daughters who love you? Very well. You can take your rose home with you. You must give it to whichever of your daughters loves you enough to come back here to live with me. And if none of them is loving and brave enough to come, be sure you shall not escape me: you shall die. Now go!"

Still clutching his rose, the merchant fled back to his waiting horse and threw himself upon it and started off in frantic haste. He had no idea of the way home, but the horse, of its own accord, took him there.

When he got home the merchant told his daughters about the failed cargo and the lost fortune and also about the enchanted palace, the Beast and the Beast's roses. His elder daughters were furious that the only present he had brought back with him was a rose for Beauty. They began quarrelling as to which of *them* should have it. But when they heard that whoever took the rose must go back to the Beast, neither wanted it, even to save their father's life.

Then Beauty took the rose and said that she would go. Her father would not consent to such a thing, although in fear for his life. Beauty did not argue, but in the middle of the night, when everyone else was asleep, she crept down to the stables to her father's horse. She mounted it and whispered in its ear: "I am sure you are a wise horse who understands everything and forgets nothing: take me, please, to the Beast's palace." The horse set off with her at once.

Beauty reached the enchanted palace before dawn. Every window of the palace was brilliantly lit, as if in celebration of her coming. She went up the agate steps, through the doors inlaid with gold, and into the great hall. Just as her father had said, every door opened before her. In one room she found a table laid: she sat down at it and delicious food and drink appeared before her, and knife and fork sprang into her hands.

While she was still eating, the whole
palace began to shake, as if with thunder: the
Beast was coming. Beauty did not run or
hide, but she was so afraid that, as the door
opened, she curtsied to the ground to avoid
seeing the Beast before her.

The Beast spoke with a great roaring voice, but not unkindly. "Beauty," he said, "you must not curtsey to me, for you are queen and mistress here. This palace and these gardens and all their delights are at your command. My only wish is that you should live here in happiness."

At that Beauty raised her eyes to him. Although the Beast looked just as her father had described, she saw that he was no longer angry.

He said: "I have one question to ask you, Beauty – the only thing I shall ever ask you. Can you love me?"

"Alas, poor Beast!" said Beauty, for already she pitied him. "How could I ever love such as you?"

At that the Beast gave a great sigh and shambled away. The next day he came to Beauty at the same time with the same question; and Beauty gave him the same answer; and every day after that.

Meanwhile, Beauty's life in the enchanted palace and its gardens was filled with delight, as the Beast had promised. She loved music, and invisible instruments played whatever she loved best. She loved animals, and silky-haired Persian kittens played around her feet; and little spaniels ran ahead of her wherever she went. In the gardens, flowers scented the air wherever she walked, especially the roses. The singing of larks outside her window woke her in the morning: and at night she fell asleep to the song of the nightingale.

Beauty would have been happy but for thoughts of her father. She knew that he must be grieving for her, believing her to be dead. So at last she asked the Beast if she could go home. "Only for three nights," she said. "Just long enough to set my father's mind at rest. Then I shall come back to you."

The Beast sighed heavily. "You can go, Beauty," he said. "But remember that I shall be lonely without you. If you stay away from me for longer than three nights, I shall begin to die of loneliness." Then he gave her a magic ring, telling her to put it by her bed before she went to sleep. In the morning she would wake where she wanted to be.

Beauty did just as the Beast told her, and woke next morning in her own room in her father's house.

The merchant was overjoyed to see his daughter again, alive and well and with wonderful stories of the Beast's enchanted palace and its delights. The two elder sisters were full of jealousy and malice. They managed to persuade Beauty to stay for one more night than she had promised, because, they said, her father needed her so much.

That fourth night she fell asleep and began dreaming at once of the Beast. She heard his voice, full of sadness: "You have not come back to me, Beauty, and I am dying of loneliness."

At once, still half-asleep, Beauty sprang out of bed and fetched the magic ring and set it by her bedside and willed herself to sleep again. This time she woke, as she had wished, in the Beast's palace.

She began immediately to search for the Beast, calling his name wherever she went. He was nowhere. She ran from the palace into the gardens, among the walks and lawns, still calling him. At last she came to a walk at the end of which played a fountain of high-glittering water; beyond it, a bower of roses.

In this bower she saw the Beast lying. She ran and knelt beside him. He could only whisper: "Beauty, I am dying ... "

"No!" she cried. "Dear Beast, you must not die, for at last I know that I love you."

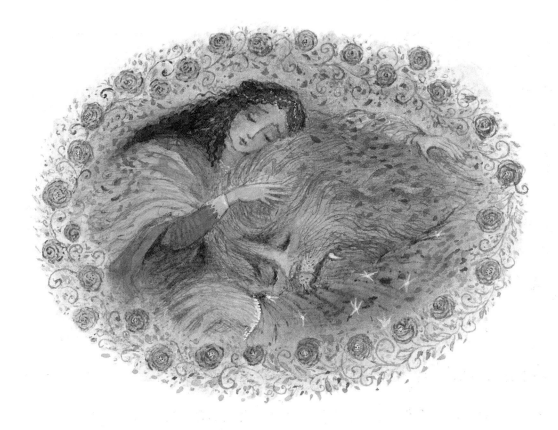

At her words the Beast began to shiver and to shimmer and to change. He rose to his feet, and as he rose he changed — changed from a Beast into a handsome young Prince.

The Prince took Beauty by the hand and spoke to her. He had a gentle and loving voice, but deep, like the Beast's own voice heard in a dream. He told her that, long ago, a wicked fairy had turned him from Prince into Beast, to remain so until someone should love him for himself alone.

"And you came, Beauty," the Prince said, "and broke the evil spell. You love me now, Beauty, and I have loved you since I first saw you. We should be married at once."

And so they were, with most magnificent celebrations. Beauty's two elder sisters were not invited to the wedding. Her father came, however, and wept for joy at his daughter's happiness. And Beauty and her Prince lived happily ever after.

180

Other titles available in the Classic Fairy Tales series:

Cinderella
Retold by Adèle Geras   Illustrated by Gwen Tourret

The Ugly Ducking
Retold by Sally Grindley   Illustrated by Bert Kitchen

Beauty and the Beast
Retold by Philippa Pearce   Illustrated by James Mayhew

Little Red Riding Hood
Retold by Sam McBratney   Illustrated by Emma Chichester Clark

Rapunzel
Retold by James Reeves   Illustrated by Sophie Allsopp

Jack and the Beanstalk
Retold by Josephine Poole   Illustrated by Paul Hess

Snow White and the Seven Dwarfs
Retold by Jenny Koralek   Illustrated by Susan Scott

Hansel and Gretel
Retold by Joyce Dunbar   Illustrated by Ian Penney

Thumbelina
Retold by Jenny Nimmo   Illustrated by Phillida Gili

Snow-White and Rose-Red
Retold by Antonia Barber   Illustrated by Gilly Marklew

Sleeping Beauty
Retold by Ann Turnbull   Illustrated by Sophy Williams

Rumplestiltskin
Retold by Helen Cresswell   Illustrated by John Howe

Goldilocks and the Three Bears
Retold by Penelope Lively   Illustrated by Debi Gliori